PASSING GUEST

Stories on Love, Kindness and Hope

IRIS MIR

Photo of the author: Manuel Outumuro

Cover design: Josep Maria Mir + Roderic Molins

These short stories are entirely a work of fiction.
The names, characters and events in this publication are fictious.
Any resemblance to real persons, living or dead, is purely coincidental.

ISBN-13: 978-1-7399979-2-2
Published by Yi Books

www.irismir.net

Contents

PASSING GUEST

Stories on Love, Kindness and Hope

Prologue: I Feel Love

This book is an experiment. And it wasn't really planned. For quite some time, I had been wanting to write about love. I wasn't sure how to do it. I found it an extremely complex topic to approach in the shape of a fictional story. Yet, I was fascinated by it. I often wondered, if love is so full of life, so essentially human, why was I finding love so difficult to grasp as the subject matter of a new book?

Love has the ability to drive us crazy. But because it emanates from our hearts, it can also give us direction. But only if we want to learn how to listen to it. Love is ever-changing. It doesn't know how to stand still because it is the result of the seemingly impossible: Two strangers finding a way to be in sync. To rise and fall together. To create a bond from the unknown. A connection that makes it very hard to run away from each other. If people are dynamic and unpredictable, love must be too… Perhaps this is why it is so attractive and scary at the same time, and the reason I was finding it so hard to write about.

Truth is, I was stuck because I was focusing on putting into words things that can't be explained, or even suggested. I was creatively approaching love the wrong way. If love can only be experienced, I must pay attention to the uniqueness of that experience. The kindness and the compassion that emanate from love and which make human relationships possible, beyond romantic love.

During the Covid-19 pandemic and the long lockdowns that we experienced in the United Kingdom, I was able to make time to do something that I love: to take to the streets and let random strangers surprise me. I sat in parks, and I spent hours walking, letting bystanders fill the gap left by the isolation that came with the imposed social distance. Certainly, my past as a journalist influenced my new lockdown ritual.

When we rush, we don't have time to experience the environment, the people we share our surroundings with. We are fully disconnected from everyone and everything that is not part of our routine. However, during the slow-paced life of the pandemic, my daily walks gave me the opportunity to go back to the beautiful feeling of paying attention to details. To how we do things, and how we deal with the most insignificant moments of our lives. These moments that we take for granted but are such an integral part of our daily lives. Small actions such as crossing the street, picking up our groceries at the shop, the way we walk, smile, cry, exercise, arrange our clothes, clean the house, read a book, wave our hand, write a note, say thank you, get mad, the way we take care of each other… the way we love! These apparently insignificant moments that we easily forget why they matter are the big storytellers of how we live life.

Likewise, I wanted to experiment with the things that are familiar to us and how they can connect us to world views that are beyond what we see as the norm. Elements from our daily lives such as our cities, our parks, a bench, our house plants, our friends, our neighbours, our books, music, schooling, the people on the streets, our families, a rooftop, the sea, the rain, the moon, the water, and ultimately storytelling - which is inherent in humankind and one of the best ways to immortalise experiences and give voice to others - can potentially connect us to others in a way that enables to explore life's possibilities beyond what is close to our known realities.

With these ideas in mind, I got out my old notes on love and I came up with a creative writing exercise. For eight weekends in a row - no excuses! - I would draft one fully fictional love story. I created some rules for myself on how to do it. I would imagine how some of the random people I saw on the streets would experience love. What would they tell me if we had the chance to have a conversation about love? Would they have any regrets? Would they be in love? Heartbroken, maybe? Were they missing someone? Would they even believe in love? What do they think about friendship? Were they feeling lonely? How do they see others?

I wondered what they would think if I told them I was dreaming a different life for them. A new future that was triggered by a new possibility of love, of compassion and kindness toward others…With this in mind, I wrote their dreamed stories almost as if it was some sort of a journalistic reportage or news column retold in the first person. Honouring their experience, their voice and the reason their hypothetical love-experience would matter to our social fabric. Their imaginary stories became a reminder of the importance of many small human acts of kindness that, for many people, were no longer available during the pandemic.

During the lockdowns, these nameless random strangers kept me company. They set my imagination free and they let me transport myself to the possibility of new and unique ways of living. They brought me closer to the life of others. Almost as if I was able to travel in time and space through their imaginary experiences. Unknowingly, they gave me hope in the midst of the pandemic and I am thankful to them.

For the same reason that this book would not be possible without the unconditional support of my good friend, Anna-Marie Savio. She selflessly offered to spend many hours of her time reading and re-reading my work, giving me valuable honest feedback. And this is how the fictional love stories motivated by those random strangers took on a dimension of their own. They deepened our friendship during the pandemic. These imaginary stories gave us both hope. They kept us going!

This book is a collection of eight fully fictional short stories on love, kindness and hope. Each one of them delves into the possibilities of finding or escaping love, where love takes many different forms and shapes. They are followed by an additional short story to commemorate International Women's Month. And a new creative piece on love that I never published before.

Passing Guest starts with a first-person introduction by an imaginary character. A woman who asks herself some questions about love. She embodies the essence behind the enigmas of love and hope that many different people I met throughout my adult life shared with me. These people all seemed to disagree on everything when it comes to describing and experiencing love. But they all clearly agreed with one simple thing: love is magic.

Some people told me once, they believed we tend to expect love to be something else, someone else, somewhere else… This is why, like the best magic tricks, we might have an act of love and kindness in front of our eyes, and we might fail to see it. Complex human beings that we are, we tend to make love complicated. So this is how this imaginary character takes on a journey of her own in which she incarnates eight different possibilities of love and life.

Her quest takes her to Hong Kong, South Korea, North Korea and neighbouring mainland China, The Democratic

Republic of the Congo, South Sudan, Uganda, Senegal, and the cities of London and Barcelona. As she tries to find her answers, she transports herself to different universes, possibilities of being and seeing, and ultimately of finding love.

With love there is hope for a better future. When we build a certain love connection - a bond of kindness - things will always feel better. There is no better hope in life than having someone by our side who is capable of making our life fuller. Soon she discovers that who she is (and who we are) can only be answered by the magic of love, which is as beautifully unique as every single one of us who makes up our diverse humanity.

Love is freedom!

BEGINNING

I, Fear

Inever quite understood why love is scarier than hate. We don't say I love you often enough. Not because we don't love the other person but because we are scared of letting the other person know how we feel about them: kind, loving, helpful, beautiful, special, honest, unique… These are words we struggle to say out loud. If people annoy us though, we will readily let them know. We will let it out because no one likes to be annoyed by someone else. Our personal space is too precious. Or is it because of pride and ego?

Why does kindness remain so scarce as opposed to anger? This question has been nagging me for a very long time. I was looking for clear, straight answers and I couldn't find them. Until one day I finally came across the answer: It's because of fear. Any show of love or kindness, in big or small measure, is a loss of control. Our feelings are exposed when our love and recognition for the other is manifested. Through our heart we reveal our true self. We have no place to hide. Our hearts don't lie. Most of the time, the stronger these feelings are, the more we want to run away from them. We must protect ourselves from love! From the other! Or else someone might break our hearts into a million pieces. And this is a horrible feeling to have. Particularly if we have been hurt before, which we all have.

The older we get, and the more we rely on reason to make choices, the more we run away from love. The relationship between love and fear permeates our souls so deeply that we tend to forget how easy it was for us to embrace love when we were children. Back then, our hearts were more aware. How or why, it didn't matter. We were just there, ready to embrace whatever came our way. We were innocent and naive. We embraced the other with love, kindness and compassion. Youth is capable of triggering those powerful passionate instincts that we need to live life in fulness.

If I ever manage to fully free myself from fear, I think I will consider it my life's biggest victory. When we free ourselves from fear, we allow ourselves to let go and to take in anything that life has in store for us. We give ourselves the chance to believe, to dream, to grow, and to be free from any reasoning that curtails our opportunity to remain true to ourselves regardless of the reality that surrounds us. To love!

Like many of us, I lost love in the past. And I am determined to understand why that happened. Because true love should never be lost. It is too scarce, too precious, too human to let it get away, to live without it. Love gives us **HOPE.** It gives us the strength to live, to believe and to keep going.

There is more to love than just the labels that we put on it and the commitments that societies expect us to subscribe to. Unconditional love takes the shape of kindness and compassion to ourselves and to others. I lost friendships and two meaningful relationships for lack of unconditional love. With all of them, when life got real, everything was lost. And that is ok. It had to be abandoned to make space for unconditional kindness and compassion from people who were willing to see my authentic self.

Life is often kind. It likes to send unique, honourable individuals our way, but our fears might take them away from us. I know romantic love is the scariest of all. But I can only say that if you are in love, flow with it and let yourself grasp this unique chance to be in **LOVE.** Because this is the most remarkable thing of all, once you allow yourself to fall in love, you don't need to do anything else. Love will take care of it and do the rest. Regardless of where this love takes you, you will only grow with it. We all will!

The essence of my story remains: I lost my first true love to fear and reason. Honourable people are scarce, so if you truly love someone (romantic, friendship, family…), free yourself from fear.

LET THEM KNOW.

#1.Metamorphosis in Hong Kong

I never planned to spend my first few days in my new city like this. Alone and trapped inside the smallest room I have ever been in. If I open my arms wide, I can touch both sides of the room. I don't even need to fully straighten up my elbows to do that. Literally, the only space available is filled with my single bed, which is placed against the wall on the left and with a small space of less than half a meter on the right. Hanging from the wall, on top of the bed, there is a small TV set. The bathroom is shared and it is located at the end of the corridor, outside my room. This is one of the hottest months in Hong Kong and despite the rain and the wind, the noisy and old aircon doesn't seem to help much to make the atmosphere inside the room less stuffy and humid. I must keep the tiny window closed otherwise I will get an indoor storm.

Tired of trying to stay awake and battling the jet lag, I keep dozing off. Sometimes, I try to stand up to see if that helps me stay awake. It is only 1pm and I must find a way to not fall asleep fully until my evening. I move my legs, I circle my ankles… but I don't seem to have space to do much more. So I give up, and I go back to laying down in bed. As if it were a dream. I know it isn't.

Suddenly, all I have in my head is the book Metamorphosis by Franz Kafka. I read it when I was a teenager because it was part of the compulsory school curriculum at the time. There was something about the story that disturbed me more than anything. It wasn't the fact that Mr. Gregor Samsa had become some sort of a disgusting insect. What stayed with me about that story was the confusion that his transformation created in himself and everyone around him: his parents, his sister, his boss and the maid. To me Kafka's story was a declaration of intentions about the fear of changing who you are and not being aware of it until it has already happened. Then, all you can do is to deal with it. I believed this was the reason they were all muddled. For them, Gregor's change had happened unannounced.

It is interesting how our minds work: my memories from the book Metamorphosis are surfacing just when I am here by myself isolated in this room on the day I have made the big move of leaving my hometown of Barcelona to start a new life in Hong Kong. I have a lot of people who love me back home, but they are confused about who I am. To them, I am a very cerebral person so they never understood why someone like myself would make the bold decision of moving to Asia with no job. Clearly, they don't know me at all. They would feel defeated if they knew the real reason I came to Hong Kong…

My mind, abruptly, shifted focus again: this is it! Gregor was secretly in love with someone. Let's be honest, being in love makes us do weird stuff. Actually, the moment we are in love, we stop being ourselves. How scary is this! So maybe this was why he became an insect. The materialisation of the metamorphosis he went through as he fell in love with that someone, who doesn't even deserve a mention in the story, but who made him turn into an insect!

At what point in time do we start doing weird stuff when we fall in love? I do not recommend to anyone to fall in love with your neighbour, particularly if he lives next door. It is torture! Everything he does, you will know. And you don't even have to see him for you to know. If he is cooking some of his delicious food, you will know! As soon as you leave your flat, the corridor will smell of his yummy stir fry. If he is going out wearing something nice after a good shower, you will also know, because the corridor will have his irresistible smell. If he comes home late, you will also know as you hear the door and you will wonder why his night ended up being a long one… When you don't want to see him, because on that day you want some privacy, then you will stumble onto him on the staircase every single time! Because sometimes the universe plays by its own rules. This is why, on the days you do want to bump into him, he will be nowhere to be found. So you will start going crazy and eventually do more weird stuff. Such as observing him walking down the street from the window in your living room. Just to realise how much you like the way he walks casually on the streets: how he swings his arms, moves his legs, turns around to check if a car is coming, or in which manner he zips up his winter jacket and adjusts his hat. If you are about to leave your flat and you sense he is also on his way out, you will rush so much to get ready to make sure you have a chance to say hi in the corridor. If on that day your senses were right and you do stumble onto him, then you will try to be natural and do more weird stuff.

At that point in time, you realise you might even end up losing your head! And if you do, how will you know that you've gone crazy? You live by yourself; no one will tell you. In fact, how will I know if I eventually lose my head for being alone in isolation in this tiny room in a city I don't even know, while it feels the world is about to end due to the torrential rain outside.

Love is a fantasy as much as the Hong Kong that lies outside this building. I can only play around with the ideas I have about this city in my head. All I did before deciding to move here two months ago was to watch the famous movie Chungking Express about two impossible love stories in which the couples involved keep doing weird stuff for the sake of love. At the time, I thought there had to be something in Hong Kong that allowed them to behave in that way so comfortably. That manner of acting weird was not just a consequence of love, it was Hong Kong! In that city, they were free to be who they were. Even if that meant acting weird. Soon enough, I started fantasising about the idea of moving to a place that was christened with the name of Fragrant Harbour due to its past as an agarwood incense trading harbour. It is romantic…

Barcelona and my neighbour feel very distant from here. The mystery of having made such a life changing decision is taking over me. How will this new life and this new city change me? Will they change me as much as my love for my neighbour did? After all, living in a new city sparks the same curiosity as love.

Now that I think about it, I don't think Gregor lost his head… I think he simply finally found himself. Becoming an insect was a metaphor for the challenge ahead of him. He had to deal with that absolute realisation: that this was who he was! The love he felt for that hypothetical someone must have been so great that it pushed him to see why he was feeling it so intensively. It was because of who he really was. The person he was hiding inside him for fear of not being normal, for not being like everyone else around him.

And this is why I am here. I want Hong Kong to drive me crazy. To make me do so much weird stuff to the point that

I become myself fully. That version of myself that feels as impossible as my love for my neighbour next door, but which is as real and weird as the mystery of making the life changing decision of moving to Hong Kong.

END

#2.Mud

It took me some time to get used to the muddy parks of London in winter. I thought mud was too messy, so I tried to avoid walking on the grass during my first two winters in this city. It felt like torture. I did not enjoy walking on pavement in the park. It made no sense to me. Pavement has always been for running and cycling but the grass is for walking.

Mud isn't for me, I used to tell myself. Let's face it. I come from warmer and drier weather, where mud is only a consequence of the occasional rain. The sun dries the earth and everything goes back to the solid terrains I was used to walking on. Mud was a little inconvenience that could be deliberately avoided. So why even bother to get my shoes dirty?

My dad, who was an international documentary maker, had a very firm view on this. He would chase interesting stories anywhere on Earth. But when it came to choosing his home base, weather was non-negotiable.

I grew up listening to my dad's stories of resilience, hope, love, dreams, fear, sadness, happiness and injustice. He was a quiet man, and he would only open up around the intimacy of a glass of good red wine. This is how he liked to talk about the inspiring people he had met around the world when shooting documentaries. Interestingly, he had this sensitivity towards others but always refused to have enough flexibility with himself to change the way he lived life. He believed that there were certain things about himself that were not up for discussion. So he kept his gift of an open mind exclusively for his passion of listening to and telling the stories of others.

The same rigidity of mind caused him to fall in love with the wrong woman: my mom. She was beautiful inside and out. They loved each other very much. My dad was convinced that she was "the one". Because he knew it to be true. A man like him could only fall in love with a woman like her. And because a woman like her was hard to find, he quickly married her. They were very young but their love would not be denied.

Because of my dad's stubbornness, he failed to see my mom's true nature. She was a good person but she was a woman of adventure. The intense love that they had for each other led her to believe, wrongly, that she was ready to slow down and become a different type of person. My dad's audacious nose for true stories failed him this time. At least, this is what he confessed to me when I turned 20 years old and he explained, for the first time, how he fell in love with her.

My dad's honesty about his love story helped me come to terms with the fact that my mom had abandoned us just a couple of years before his confession. I was an adult then, and ready to experience life and love differently. I had promised myself that the fear of falling in love with the wrong person would never happen to me. That I was a different person to my dad. That I had learnt from his story and I would not be that stubborn.

This is how I came to believe that I was a truly open and flexible person. And that such attributes would help me with love. I tried very hard to make sure that I stored that image of myself deep in my body. I told myself that there was obviously no such thing as "the one". Doing so would set me free from making the same mistakes my dad had made in life and love, I hoped.

However, love, for me, took on a life of its own. I fell in love with very interesting men. They were all very different from each other. Although they loved me very much, they did not know how to be with me permanently. At some point, they all decided to lie to me and, eventually, leave.

Heartbroken and sick of unreliable men, I decided to move to London. I had no clue what I was doing. Me living in this terrible weather! If my dad had not passed away the year before, he would surely have reminded me that a true home base must always be built in warmer and drier weather.

Perhaps he was right. But I did not care. I was on a quest to dare my past. If I wanted to break this curse, I told myself, I had to irrevocably defy the integrity of my being. Only in this way could I find durable and permanent love with a man who was able to commit to staying by my side.

I strongly resisted the idea that at some point mud would need to be a part of my life if I were to remain in London. Stubborn me had to come to terms with the inconvenience of muddy shoes if I wanted to walk through life on a different terrain.

As much as I wanted to be flexible, I just couldn't. So I gave myself time. There are so many things to do in London that I wrongly believed I could always make plans with friends in many different places that were mudproof. So why rush?

People in London cherish their parks. Strange people, I told myself. How is it possible that even when it is freezing cold, gloomy or even rainy they like to hang out in them? Londoners are the masters of adaptation, I thought. How come they have a reputation for being headstrong then? Adaptation required flexibility! Many of my dad's stories of resilience taught me so.

Being so resilient to this weather surely teaches them something over time. Probably there were a few things I could learn from them and their relationship with the muddy parks in winter… but I resisted. The mud, remember the mud, such an inconvenience, I silently repeated in my mind. I did not know, though, that there was something I would never be able to escape: true love.

So when I met Adam, and he took me out on a date for the first time for a walk in the park, I knew I was done with my mud free commitment. I did not panic too much yet. I planned to stay alert so that we could stick to the paved road and avoid walking on the grass. Messy, muddy shoes would be avoided with this little strategy. After all, I barely knew him. Why on earth would I go through such an inconvenience to flirt with a stranger?

Halfway through our first date we were already walking on the grass. He was becoming the best man I had ever met. I knew I was in trouble, and I was not ready for that. But there we were, with muddy shoes learning about each other, trying to feel each other.

Adam and I made Sunday morning walks in the park our private weekly ritual. Walking on the muddy grass gave us the intimacy new couples seek to face the fears of a potential new love. My shoes got muddy and I had to completely let go of that. For the very same reason, at some point, I would have no choice but to surrender to the love I felt for him. I pretended for as long as I could that the stickiness of love would never reach my heart. I wasn't ready for that. He wasn't either. So we agreed to take it slow. To see where things were going. This was how we found our own way to make the inconvenience of unplanned love, convenient. After all, my surrendering to muddy walks was already a big step.

The only physical evidence he left behind every week were the small chunks of dried mud that dropped from our shoes on the staircase on our way up to my flat after our Sunday walks. There they remained as a reminder of our ephemeral love. Until the man that cleaned the building would come on Thursdays and sweep it away. The wiped clean floor became a confirmation of my presumed ability to control the fate of our relationship.

There was one big thing my dad and I did not have in common. I am an extremely superstitious person. I believe in fate and signs from the Universe. This was the only thing, perhaps, that my dad never accepted about me. His career in storytelling brought him into contact with stories of personal struggle in which, according to him, fate and superstitions had no place. Real, raw life was all that made our existence true. His job was to let the world know about them.

Since I learnt about the fate of my parents' love story, I often thought that their reluctance to embrace the beauty of the inexplicable things in life was at the root of the failure of their marriage. I wondered if, when they met, they both put so much effort into finding a reasonable explanation for the love that they felt for each other, that, even though they thought they were being led by their hearts, it was, in fact, their minds that were telling them that theirs was an ever-lasting love.

How would things have gone if my parents had let some of the magic of life get in the way of their decision to be together? Perhaps if they had followed their intuition, they would have seen that my mom was a free spirit unable to commit to a family.

Days, weeks and months passed by. So did our weekly Sunday walks in the park. We never dared to bring the nature of our emotionally convenient romantic arrangement up again. I consciously allowed myself to fall in love with Adam. It felt safe to do it this way. If there was no commitment, then there was nothing he could run away from and hurt me. On the other hand, if there was hope for a true, permanent love in the future, then he was worth my heart. Regardless, my nose told me he was the best man I had ever met.

I sometimes wondered if there was a message behind the meaning of our love and the mud that Adam left behind. Can we escape love in the same way that I had been determined to escape mud? We can escape our past - learn to live in different ways - but we can't escape true love. My parents didn't. If the mud was being swept away from my building's staircase on Thursdays, and on Sundays Adam was still showing up for our muddy walks, then it clearly meant that he was there to stay.

My mom never lied to my dad. She just reached a point when she had to go. For the first time, I realised my dad was never mad at my mom. He loved her even after she had left us and until his death. Because, since the first day they met, he had understood her. He was there to see her. And his love for her was all that mattered. My mom wasn't the wrong woman, after all. They were right for each other in their own way.

But was Adam there to see me? I will never find out. Yesterday, as he had done every Thursday for the last two years, the cleaner swept away Adam's mud for the very last time. It was difficult watching the remains of his mud fading away on the staircase. Getting smaller and smaller every day as the neighbours kept stepping on it. On our Sunday walk the week before, he decided to end it. Immediately, and for the first time, I told him that I loved him. It didn't change anything. To him, what we had was never going anywhere. For me, he had become my first true love; the one I wanted to commit to.

The brittle chunks of mud he left behind on his last visit to my flat were a reminder that I never got the chance to truly know Adam. They were a memory of the parts of him that I missed. And of the small bits of him that will stay inside me. Somewhere in that place that can't be reached or erased.

They say that if you truly love someone, you have to let them go. The same advice applies if you are the one willing to move on and leave someone behind. What a contradiction in life! To my superstitious mind, the clean floor on that dreadful Thursday evening was a sign that, for the first time, I had experienced a different type of broken heart.

Obviously, not all love can be swept away like crumbling mud. I was grateful to have had the chance to experience him. I just missed the chance to get to know him deeply. The chance to be with him without any boundaries. To be free with him. Free from the fear of loving him. Unfortunately, only commitment would have removed those boundaries. Without it, we had to enforce an emotional distance to keep things casual. To make sure our hearts did not go crazy. To not spiral into love and then realise we had to do something about it before we were both ready.

Was it the mind that was keeping us apart? Was it the body? Was it the irrational fear of the present moment or the fear of painful disappointments from the past that were stored in our hearts?

Mud free again but filled with a love I couldn't explain or do anything about, I finally understood that there was really no love spell that I needed to break. Perhaps this was what my dad was trying to tell me when he rejected my superstitions: nothing is forever. And all that mattered to him and my mom was the ability to commit to the love they had right there and then. Theirs was a love led by courage, without fear of the future or the impermanence of life.

Nothing will ever change the fact that, regardless of the outcome, there are loves that last forever. And for the beauty that this entails, we should never let go of them. My mom and dad never did and this is how, in their own way, they had been perfect for each other.

If only Adam and I had given our hearts permission to get muddy and embrace the mess, we might have discovered that, whatever happened, it could always be swept clean. But no sweeping will ever erase the memory of a love that could have been but wasn't.

END

#3. Water

I used to arrive late at school every single day. Some people might think that happened because I was a dreamer or easily distracted; unable to get to places on time. They were right. My imagination kept me busy, and I was a dreamer. But that wasn't the reason I was late to school. Growing up, I had to walk two hours a day to bring water to my family. The bucket I carried on top of my head was heavy. The terrain was dusty, and my flip flops made walking long distances difficult. Sometimes I would just go barefoot. I felt I walked faster that way, hoping I might manage to get to school a bit earlier. The muddy roads during the wet season were too slippery without shoes. So I mostly did that only in summer.

Standing now on this shore, overlooking the vast Atlantic, I remembered thinking how water was the element holding back my dreams but also the element that brought me here. Every single day, as I was regretting being late to school, I was dreaming about how it would feel to swim in the open waters of the ocean. To be one with water rather than water being something scarce that was keeping me away from a future I wanted. Water was taking my freedom away.

My mom often told me she never wanted me to end up like her. And that water would lead me to freedom. Fetching water for my family allowed her to have more time to work on our little farm and make some money from selling the produce. She promised me that one day I would be free to be who I wanted to be. Sometimes, I think my mom should have been born somewhere else or at another time. Whenever, wherever, but in an environment in which she could have fully embraced who she was. Rather than poverty taking away her aspirations and her chance to shine. Her determination was one of the few memories that I had of her. It kept me going.

There was another way that water prevented me from living a full life: armed conflict.

I made it to the Bidibidi refugee camp in northern Uganda as one of the many South Sudanese fleeing across the border, and arriving en masse, since 2016. People who are used to peace and stability often reject wishful thinking. They believe that if you dream too much you are wasting your time. You are not being realistic. If they were right, I - and the more than 230 thousand refugees who fled to northern Uganda- would have never made it here. And without my dreams, I would never have left it.

In the five years I spent in Bidibidi, I saw the camp expand into five areas to accommodate the ever-growing flow of refugees. The majority of them were women with children. I was not that lucky. I came here by myself. I had to run away from my village in South Sudan without even knowing where my mom was. I had to leave everything behind to save my life. I went through all sorts of horrors in the forest to make it here. I kept telling myself that one day I would swim in the vast open ocean where water is never scarce.

Bidibidi is not a settlement of people, but one of hope. Architects, accountants, journalists, farmers, business owners... we all shared the same land. Some hoped to go back to South Sudan. Others felt that, with time, this improvised city of Bidibidi would become a new home from where they could start building new businesses, new dreams, new families and new futures.

Their determination inspired me, and I tried not to let the empty promises and broken dreams of some of the other girls make me give up on my dreams of the ocean.

Most of the girls who arrived here without their families were hoping to get married quickly so that they could get support. Mostly by way of food and some money to pay for emergency medical treatments, if needed. Marriage always went hand in hand with unwanted babies and dropping out of school. Having access to an education was possibly the only safe way out of that camp.

When it rained in South Sudan, my mom and I used to collect as much extra water as we could. We filled up all the empty buckets, as well as our drums. I would always stand in the rain, my eyes closed, and imagine how it would feel to swim in the vast ocean. My mom believed in freedom as much as I did. And she only told me about her and my dad one day when she joined me in the rain. She put her two hands together, palms facing up, making a little bowl of flesh. She waited for a bit, in silence, until her hands filled with water. Then she explained to me that water was as precious as love. That life was not possible without either. She slowly pulled her hands apart. Some of the water melted with the rain and fell onto the ground. When she brought her two hands back together, the rain filled up that imaginary well again. My mom's hands filled with the joy of rain became my own metaphor for love. That day, she finally explained to me how she made the brave call of divorcing my dad. He was a good man, but she was not happy. She was not married because of love. With him, water was constantly leaking from her hands. She had no hope; her heart was empty.

In Bidibidi, I finally fully understood what my mom was trying to tell me. That freedom was good, but that love was more important. And as much as I wanted to swim in the vast ocean, I should also have a heart filled with love. A heart that doesn't leak with sorrow.

Some of the women I met in Bidbidi would have agreed with my mom. They all had different life experiences, but they were committed to holding us together. These brave communities of women refugees reminded us of the importance of going to school every day, of taking care of each other so that we could prevent rape and all sorts of harassment that were also part of the life at the camp. They were using their hard-won freedom to set us free. They were doing that with the same love and care that my mom was holding the rainwater in her hands just two days before I had to leave it all behind in South Sudan.

Today I am here in Dakar, Senegal's capital, remembering all the women who filled our hearts with hope. Reminding us that we had a future and that Bidibibi was not necessarily the end of our flight but the beginning of a new life that could be as full with water as the vast ocean. One day, I will become a writer and I will tell our stories.

As I swim in the abundance of water off Dakar's shores, I take on a new dream. Finding the love that my mom never had with my dad. The one that can contain as much rain as was needed. Just like our drums did in South Sudan when lack of water, war and conflict were threatening to take away the freedom in our hearts.

END

#4.Love, Books, Solitude

I used to have better handwriting… What happened to it? I am not sure. I guess my obsession for note taking is to blame for this. It is funny how life works! My devotion to taking quick notes about everything I see around me, and that inspires me, is the cause of my decaying penmanship. There is a reason for that: When I see or think about something very revealing there is no time to waste. Thoughts are powerful but at the same time they are very disappointing. They come and go as they please. We have less control over them than we want. Particularly when we talk about inspiration. Immediately we have to get our pens and notebooks and immortalise them. Or else they'll go away forever, leaving us alone and helpless. In such an extreme situation, the priority is to put down on paper anything that is in our heads in that moment. How neat it looks is secondary. The idea of a potential new story, in itself, takes precedence and we should never let it go.

However, I keep thinking I should do something about it. If I ever become a writer and I have to sign books, I don't want people to think that my handwriting is not good enough for someone who works with words. They will never know the story behind it, so they will probably assume my handwriting is just poor.

My note taking obsession was the reason Naoki and I met. I was doing one of my inspiration rituals by which I would go to the park next to my flat in London and walk around in big circles on the grass. Sometimes, I listen to music or podcasts. Other times, I let my imagination run wild while I observe the behaviour of the people around me. That day, I happened to be listening to my breakup playlist. A collection of music that I only play if I am, obviously, going through a breakup. It has over six hours of songs on it and it keeps growing. I add a new title whenever I hear a song that reminds me of the pain of a broken heart. My rule is that I can only listen to the playlist when I suffer from heartbreak. However, I always allow myself to add any new song if I feel that it has a melody that, for some reason, deserves a spot on this list. Perversely, I then wish that there will be no need for me to listen to this playlist again in the future, and that the new song will remain there unheard forever.

On the day Naoki and I met, 'How Can You Mend a Broken Heart' by Al Green was the song that brought me up short. I had been playing it on a loop for a few days and, suddenly, as part of the magic of writing, I felt I needed to write something about it. I am not sure what it was that I did at that particular moment which attracted Naoki's attention in such a powerful way. He immediately saw me in the distance. As he approached me, he looked very interested in what I was doing. I had to ask him to wait a bit. No way was I going to let my thoughts get away just to answer to a stranger. I had to risk being rude. He did a very good job of standing there, silently, while I tried to capture everything I had in my mind at that moment.

The ability of my brain to multitask, reminded me quickly about my poor handwriting. And as I was hastily scribbling notes, I twisted my shoulder a bit and inclined the angle of my notebook. I did not want my poor handwriting to be the first thing Naoki found out about me. I was curious about him too, despite my being busy with taking notes. As soon as I put away my notebook, he asked again:

"I am sorry, but I am very intrigued. You look so beautiful taking notes with so much determination and love".

And then he added:

"Are you a writer?"

I froze for a few seconds not knowing what to answer. Could I consider myself a writer? Finally, I dared to tell him that I was halfway through writing my first novel but that I was not a writer, yet. He disagreed, saying that finishing it will not make me a writer. And because he had never seen anyone taking notes the way I did, to him I was a writer, period.

He joined me for the rest of my walk, and we talked casually about ourselves and our lives in London. Before I headed back home, he asked for my notebook and my pen. Hesitantly, I handed it over to him, wondering why I was trusting a stranger with my notebook full of precious notes. That was too intimate! And yet I gave it to him. He was careful to show me that he was willing to respect the privacy of those notes. He flipped it over and opened the last page, on which he wrote his name and phone number in an elegant, flowing script.

It took me more than a week to find the courage to call him. Before that, I had spent quite a few hours looking at his name and phone number in my notebook. I was wondering who this man was and what his peculiar and fine handwriting could tell me about him.

Breakups are painful because they transport us to the depths of an unbearable solitude. One that drags us into places we don't often want to go to. We question ourselves, the integrity of our being and the true nature of the love that we feel for the person that has just left us. Is anything real, after all? Or are we even real? Are we sure of who we are and what we want? Getting out of that dark place is something we can only do on our own.

Since I was very little, books have been the place in which I managed to find and see myself from different angles. They were a window onto other ways of being and seeing. Learning about them made me feel less alone and, therefore, more myself. Stories brought to light my own aspirations, happiness, confusion and suffering, ending the exhausting feeling of isolation that we sometimes have to endure in life.

I have this little secret I never shared with any of my lovers. It is one of the few memories I have as a child. At school, in our classroom, we had a bookshelf with the books available for our reading. Every year, we were supposed to borrow some of them to nurture and grow our identity as future readers. My favourite moment had always been when I had to pick a new book. I remember most of the kids would stand in front of the shelves browsing. Paying attention to the cover, the amount of words it had inside, drawings if applicable, the length of the book, etc. For me, the most important thing was the smell of the book! Part of my browsing process included opening the book and bringing it close to my nose to smell it and feel it. Something challenging of course because, even for a child, this was a very private act that I would have preferred to do in solitude for fear of what the other kids would think about such a strange ritual. Hiding was not an option. The bookshelf was located in the corner of the classroom and I always felt very exposed.

Children tend to fool themselves that they are not being watched when, in fact, they are. And this was exactly what I did with those books. If I found a title that caught my attention, I would open it up and smell it before making my final choice. Through their smell, the books came alive inside me, waiting for the magic to carry me away when I delved into the story later. A very instinctive process for the innocent and pure mind of a kid.

For some reason, every time I fell in love with a man, my mind transported me back to this private moment of my childhood smelling books. As if I was making a connection between doing something secret, like falling in love, and the exposure that it takes to show myself to the person I like. Perhaps this is the reason I was feeling so scared of becoming a writer. Love, as much as books, is a legacy that stays within us. They are both stories that have been lived and experienced. They change us thanks to the other person that is reading us and feeling us.

Despite Naoki's beautiful handwriting, he believed he had no potential as a writer. He said he had other gifts. Yet, he still thought of me as a writer. He loved books and stories as much as I did. And this is how our relationship started growing as we shared books with each other and spent hours talking about them. This ritual gave me the confidence I was lacking to continue writing my first book. The breakup with my ex made me doubt myself so much, that I panicked every time I picked up my pen.

Loving someone and writing are exercises of solitude. There is nothing lonelier than loving in secret. Which we all do for a very long time until we are able to share it. To say it! Before we can do that, love needs to remain private so that it doesn't become real before we are ready to give all that we are to the other person.

With Naoki, I experienced an outburst of creativity. I did not even know where it was coming from. I was writing in solitude as I was loving him in solitude. I was in fear of my feelings for him as much as I was in fear of the things that I was discovering about myself while writing my book. These were things I thought I would never be able to say, feel or write. I was, inevitably, falling in love with Naoki.

There are things that we know just because we know them. They are so clear to us because they make sense to us only. They just feel right! And the reason they feel right inside us can be found in the environment around us.

My handwriting stopped being an issue for me the day I decided to start leaving little notes inside the books that Naoki was sharing with me. They were very innocent, and they never hinted at my love for him. I wanted him to know me better without my having to explain myself. They were little traces of the most intimate self that I was exposing to him camouflaged under the wisdom of other people's stories. Sometimes, I would just use a small piece of paper to write a comment on something I had read on a book that I found interesting. Or a memory of something that I had done or seen in the past that was somehow linked to the story I was reading. His books became my books and the other way around. We bought books for each other and we shared each other's shelves. There was more intimacy in our book sharing ritual than in anything we were doing together face to face.

Soon I discovered that being a writer meant being true to myself. To connect deep inside myself and my surroundings. Something that I couldn't do on my own. Love and writing were slowly becoming an act of sharing. Consequently, I found that writing and loving is never lonely, nor a real secret. Writing is a form of love. Love for yourself, your story, your community, the strangers and the readers you will never meet. The solitude of books and love only comes to an end when we make space in our hearts for that connection to happen.

And this is how, eventually, my skills as a writer, as much as my love for Naoki, stopped being an exercise of validation. Loving him and writing became purely about me. An expansion of myself and a manifestation of who I am. When we write, we dream. And soon enough, I started dreaming about the moment my book would be published. And how I would celebrate with Naoki. For the first time in my life everything made sense. It all felt right. This is a feeling that can't be the outcome of just my imagination, I used to tell myself. It had to be real. As real as my feelings for Naoki. There was nothing that excited me more than dedicating my novel to him.

He had become such an important part of my journey, that the words I would write to thank him had to match the kindness that he had brought into my life. As the publication of my book grew nearer, and every time inspiration came my way, I drafted different combinations of words of kindness for Naoki. Until I found the perfect dedication to him. As soon as the first author copies arrived, I wrote it down, surprisingly, without caring much about the quality of my handwriting. "To Naoki, for ending my solitude in love and writing".

There are things that we do in life that we should never stop doing. There are other things that we need to stop doing for a while to question if this is something that we really want. If they are something that makes us who we are. There are other things we have to stop pursuing altogether so that we can follow a different path.

But what happens with love? And with my love for Naoki? What about Naoki himself? The same fear of forgetting ideas and stories that led to my voracious note taking, made me wonder about Naoki's feelings for me. Was he going through a similar transformation to myself? And was he willing to embrace it? What if he did not love me? The answer to all of this wasn't love, though, but solitude. Naoki had his own story to deal with. He loved me and he wanted me. He was proud of me and didn't want to lose me. But his was a different path to explore.

Before I managed to thank him for all he had done for me, for seeing me and believing in me, he left me. And there his copy of my book, with my poor but proud handwriting in it, remains on my bookshelf hoping that someday there will be a chance for me to end Naoki's solitude and for us to finally be together.

END

#5.The Bench

Benches are the ultimate equaliser; they are pieces of furniture designed to provide a public space for fairness, ensuring all who sit on them are equal as they sit down, talk and connect. They are bigger than chairs so that they can fit more than one person. Regardless of their occupants' walks of life, benches are unique spots where people meet and share the city; share their lives. In London, I have seen people doing all sort of things on them: lovers hug, kiss, smile, cuddle and seduce each other. Strangers share benches while they read books. Mothers and fathers rest as they keep an eye on their children. Some might have lunch, others drinks… There are people who like to sit down and listen to music or to talk on the phone. Or just simply close their eyes and feel the sun on their faces. Smokers use benches to indulge their vice. Friends make confessions to each other and rough sleepers sometimes have no other choice but to make benches their home… Surely, benches see tears and joy, love and despair; and a lot of solitude!

A big part of my job as a lawyer is to pay attention to how people talk and express themselves. What does their silence tell us? Or how do they share an idea to try to win an argument? Whether in my professional capacity or in private, I observe them while sitting on a bench. My job explains my daily attachment to a bench, and how I have developed the habit of paying attention to people sitting on the benches of London. What made them take that pause in that precise instant? To pick that spot to halt their journey; to rest in the freedom of a public space?

There is one woman who captivated me. I have been seeing her every single day on my way to work. She usually sits on the same bench in the Bethnal Green Gardens Park, around 8.30am. She is on the left corner of the bench, to her right she has a cup of takeaway coffee and a notebook on her legs. She doesn't look unhappy, but she is not at peace.

From a distance, I can see that the notebook already has some notes on it. Is she always staring at the same page? Or is it a different one every day? All I know is that when I pass by her she is never writing. She is sitting down in a way that reminds me of my daily job: observing people. She is paying attention to bystanders, with a shy expression on her face and a smile that is holding something back. Is it pain, joy, fear, love, confusion? Or is it the bitter smile of disagreement I wear at work when I have to confront the outcome of unjust rulings? I know she is lonely. This is a trait I can spot very easily because I am lonely too. The first time I paid attention to her was when I noticed her shouting, as if she was talking to herself. She was agitated and she was waving the notebook in her hand…

∞

Rosa! My name is Rosa! I shouted loudly in the middle of the park. A man wearing a suit and a briefcase turned around. I felt ashamed for talking to myself so loudly. I quickly sat down and tried to calm myself by drinking my coffee. It didn't work. In tears, I read his words again:

We never told each other our names. I am Jacob and this is my story:

I have been sitting on this bench every single day, since I knew I was going to be deported back to Jamaica. I came to the UK when I was a baby, with my mom. I lived here my entire life. But I was never given the chance to get proper papers. And this is the reason my time to go has come.

I refuse to let anger and hate take over me. This notebook is proof that people are kind. Since my deportation notice, I have been taking daily notes of any gestures of love and kindness from strangers. This notebook confirms that alone we are nothing and that solitude only exists when we are made invisible. When we are stripped of our place in the community, like I was.

I fell in love with you, but I never dared to tell you because I don't stand a chance of staying. Your stories helped me feel less alone. Thank you for seeing my solitude, stopping by and sitting by my side.

With a knot in my chest, I repeated my name in silence, inside of me, over and over again: Rosa! My name is Rosa! I was hoping he could hear me. As if saying my name would bring him back or allow us to be together. I will never forgive myself for not listening to him and being the only one talking all the time. Being too busy with my own solitude.

Jacob and I met for the first time during the last few weeks of spring. I liked to spend my mornings at the park, getting some fresh air before I got trapped by my usual office environment. Being surrounded by strangers made me feel more alive. Jacob liked to sit on that bench for a reason, but he never told me why. And I never asked. I used to pass by, and he would only lift his gaze from his notebook to have a quick look at me. I was curious about him until I finally decided to sit down by his side.

"You look sad. Is everything alright?" he asked.

His question surprised me. Why would he care? Perhaps he remembered me from my daily walks. Who knows!

"I feel alone. I just lost a friend" I told him.

He closed his notebook and put it away inside his backpack. It was the first time I saw him do that. He remained silent. I still don't know why I started sharing with him the reason behind my solitude. The betrayal of an old friend, the loneliness I felt every time I wanted to talk to her, knowing that I couldn't do that anymore, that she was gone. The disappointment that came with it. My loss of faith in people.

Listening is all that Jacob did for three weeks in a row, every single morning before I went to work. The same three weeks that I know now were the last few days he had left in this country.

I was so lost in my own thoughts, so desperate for love, that I never bothered to ask anything about him. He was kind, loving and caring. And without saying anything, only by offering to listen, he reminded me that grace was the best way to pass through life, disappointments and injustice.

His notebook, the only legacy that I had from him, was witness to this. On his last day at the park before his forced departure, he left the notebook for me to find. From that bench, he was spreading his own justice. His was decent and fair; purely human. One by one, in very neat handwriting he kept track of people's acts of love and compassion. He refused to lose hope.

∞

"May I sit down?" the man wearing a suit and a briefcase asked me on his way to work.

I nodded.

He remained quiet for quite a long time. Until he finally dared to ask:

"What is it in this notebook? I am sorry but I noticed you sit here every single morning."

"I notice you pass by this bench every single day. You look sad. Is everything alright?" I asked him instead, ignoring his question about my notebook.

"I am sad. I've lost hope" he answered.

"Well, you are sitting on the bench of hope", I quickly told him.

He laughed a bit sarcastically as he added, "At work, I sit on the bench of disapproval".

After a little pause, he continued, "I am a lawyer. I support the members of the Windrush generation. I failed someone. A good man who worked in this country for many years. But who never saw justice, like many other people from the Caribbean who live here."

He paused as he caught his breath, "his name is Jacob."

∞

END

#6.Rules

Have you ever had the feeling of being watched? Not by a stranger or a spy... being watched by the people in your life. Almost as if they are sitting on the back seat of your car, watching you drive through life. They love you; they support you. They believe in you massively! But deep inside them, they still think your choice might not be the best one. Or the one they would make. Maybe you are pursuing a job they would never want for themselves. Maybe you have dreams they find scary... or boring! Maybe they don't like your partner, or lover. Not because of that person's character. But because they would not choose that person for themselves.

Maybe they disagree with how you live life. Most likely, they will enjoy that back seat riding the most when they see you fall in love. Then they might even grab the popcorn, while they enjoy the show.

They will be happy at first. Falling in love is one of the most beautiful things, albeit scary. As soon as they know more details about your romance, chances are they will support you, but be wary. Particularly if you are falling in love outside of the usual terms: if you choose to flow with it. With no guarantees of what the outcome will be. If you choose to trust that all that you have with that person so far is happening for a reason. Sometimes, love requires you to travel a journey of no questions and no answers. A journey of no rules.

They will laugh with you as you share the ups and downs. The nonsense, as well as the passionate anecdotes, the funny bits, and the tears. They will be excited that you are living a love story that looks like a movie. They will be scared for you, too. If you get it wrong, you'll have to deal with a broken heart. At some point, they will start shifting their mindset: if you can't get guarantees right now, you better walk away from it. You are getting too emotionally involved.

So there it is! If love can't be forever guaranteed, don't go down that road. Why love another person if you can't be fully sure it will be forever? Honestly, who can be sure that any form of love, or life, for that matter, will actually be forever?

At some point, you have to take the leap. Explore and see. Give time for that chance encounter, that seemed impossible in the first place, to become whatever it needs to become. Things take time, particularly when it comes to two different people. But of course, if we see love as a hallmark that we have to achieve as part of our predictable lives then, yes, we are in a hurry! This is when I can understand why your popcorn friends will not agree with the idea of waiting or giving the space to the relationship to flourish at its own pace. To see if that impossible love, is possible.

My friends like to call it: to take it slow. And they don't like it because it has no rules. According to them, relationships need to be bound by clear terms and conditions. They have to have a proper label; be clearly framed and recognised. Anything else outside this scope is a waste of time, and not smart.

Chung-Hee was the only person who understood why the situation upset me, even though he had never tried popcorn before nor been to a movie theatre. He was born in rural North Korea, in Yŏmju County. This small town is located far away from the privileged life of the capital, Pyongyang, from where the repressive apparatus of the regime operates. His was a life of austerity. Yet, he considered himself a lucky person. During the famine that killed millions of North Koreans, in the 1990s, when the state's rationing regime fell apart, his family managed to find a way to survive. Like many fellow North Koreans, they broke the rules, became creative and made some money. Chung-Hee's family even went further than that. His dad packed his stuff and smuggled himself into bordering mainland China, right at the other end of the Yalu river, not too far from their hometown. He was determined to come back with more money and newly acquired skills. In the meantime, Chung-Hee saw his mom becoming some sort of an entrepreneur. At first, she was bartering anything in exchange for food. Soon, she started finding ways to make some more money, by selling some of the little possessions they had left at home. Chung-Hee's dad was one of the lucky defectors who was never caught and managed to safely make his way back to North Korea. He was changed, though. In China, he had witnessed a different world with possibilities and opportunities. He knew he couldn't let his wife and children go back to the life of poverty imposed by the secretive regime. So he made the commitment to make and save money so that his son, Chung-Hee could cross the border and defect to South Korea with his two sisters, when they were older.

Chung-Hee grew up hearing the stories that his dad told him about the different lifestyle he could expect outside of North Korea. But his dad never told him about the freedom of love. This is something he learnt from the South Korean movies he acquired on the black market.

I met Chung-Hee inside a safe house in the Chinese north eastern region of Liaoning. He was brought over by the group of people my organisation works with to help North Koreans defect to South Korea.

Something was different about him compared to other defectors I had met before. He was scared and disoriented. The journey was long and he had never left his home town before. But I could tell there was something else about him.

He was free. And he did not need to be safe in South Korea to feel that way.

We were keeping the lights low. Staying quiet. We did not want to raise any suspicions. There were rumours of an increasing number of raids by Chinese soldiers. China was becoming less tolerant with defections. If we were caught, they would send Chung-Hee back to North Korea where he would risk ending up in a slavery camp or even executed. Defectors are normally used to darkness. Outside of Pyongyang, most of the towns are pitch black at night due to the poor electricity supply in the country.

A few hours after our first meal together, he approached me. "Tell me about love" he said.

This is a question I had never had before. I had been asked about life in a modern country like South Korea and how it felt to live in freedom. This was the first time I was asked about love.

"Why love?" I asked him.

"Love is freedom" he answered.

I remained silent for a while. To me, love had become a trap. Hesitantly, I told him that I had lost the man I loved because I couldn't handle the pressure of living a romance everyone disapproved of, and thought was impossible. Including my family.

"Well, everyone in my family disapproved of me leaving North Korea. And here I am" he interrupted.

After the famine, an informal market economy had surfaced in North Korea. His parents were better off and slowly their vision of having their children defecting faded away.

Chung- Hee believed money and the hope of better life opportunities was clouding their judgement. They couldn't see their urge to be free anymore. And they wanted their children to stay by their side, to remain North Koreans and see the possibility of the nation flourishing.

His sisters quickly agreed. They were dragged into the wrong dream of marriage and children, under the misleading idea of a stable life in North Korea.

Chung-Hee had different aspirations. He wanted freedom more than anything. He wanted love. During the two years he had been planning his escape, he had to fight the resistance of his family and their fears for him. He was told that what he aspired to was impossible.

His family was so strict with Chung-Hee's dreams for freedom that he started fearing they might report him to the authorities in an attempt to sabotage his escape. So he left the house one night without saying goodbye, while everyone was sleeping.

Chung-Hee hid in the forest for two days before it was safe for him to cross the border. He knew that if he successfully became a South Korean, he would never be able to go back to North Korea under the current regime.

After hearing Chung-Hee's story, I felt helpless. I had the freedom he was longing for, but had not used it wisely.

My family was wealthy. I knew they would never approve of my marrying a man that would not give our family its proper status. My professional aspirations were also not worthy of a lady. But I had the freedom to make the impossible, possible, and that included the freedom of love.

My parents had done a good job of sending me to Australia to get a good education and broaden my mind so that I could be a better wife. Under that idea, if I had to work before getting married, it had to be a reputable office job.

I did not want any of this. When I was in Sydney, I had met some friends working with organisations advocating for freedom in repressive countries. North Korea was one of them. Perhaps, driven by my own desire for freedom away from my repressive and conservative parents, I decided once I returned to Seoul, I would join an NGO to help North Korean defectors escape the country. So that they could be in charge of their own future.

It never occurred to me that love would be such an integral part of this freedom they were risking their lives for. I guess I took love for granted, as much as my popcorn friends who, like my family, thought my life was a journey of daring and honourable choices, but full of disappointing outcomes.

The love that Chung-Hee witnessed in those South Korean movies planted a seed of hope inside him that was too strong for him to let go. This is how he learnt that love is an act of the contradictory ideas of rebellion and acceptance; very much a part of his life and his family's in North Korea.

The balance between rebellion and acceptance made them break the rules for their own benefit to survive the famine and find a stable livelihood. In time, that stability ended their thirst for rebellion, and they accepted that life was good enough for them to settle and stop taking any more risks, like the defection of their children.

For me, the same acceptance trap kept me away from the freedom to choose love. The freedom to choose to escape with the man I wanted because that might have meant losing my family. He was a foreigner, an Australian. And I was supposed to marry only a Korean and stay in the country to breed children and take care of both my parents and my husband. I traded my freedom to choose love for the acceptance of others. My way to make up for that mistake, for losing the best man I had ever met, was to help others find freedom. In the case of Chung-Hee, to get him safely to South Korea so that he could finally find the freedom to love that he was once told was impossible.

As for me, I was left with no hope. I rebelled and left my family behind so that I could finally be free; ready to flow, to love, to live without rules… but knowing that the man I wanted was the man I had lost. The one I couldn't have and the one I couldn't forget.

END

#7. Milo's Plants

There is a massive tropical forest in Africa that spans across Cameroon, Gabon, the Republic of the Congo, Equatorial Guinea, the Democratic Republic of the Congo, and the Central African Republic. I was a child when my granddad used to tell me stories about this magnificently rich place that is home to tens of millions of local and indigenous peoples. He called it the lungs of Africa and this is how I have always remembered it.

My grandad never had access to higher learning. As a young child, living through the civil war in our country, Spain, he obtained only a rudimentary education. But his eagerness to learn about the world around him was never suppressed by the cruelty of his circumstances. He found ways to learn and discover real stories and facts about our planet all on his own.

Probably the one that astonished him the most was the Congo Basin. To make these stories easier to understand for a young child, he always avoided using the real name of what is the second largest tropical rainforest in the world –500 million acres-. He wasn't so much impressed by its size, though, but by its richness. And at over 50 000 years old, the Congo Basin is truly ancient. But these were all complicated numbers for a child, so he kept them to himself.

His marvellous imagination and sharp storytelling left a deep impression on me and the memory of this magical forest never left me. My grandad shared stories of hope and resilience of the communities inhabiting those lands. He made a big effort to make me understand that the richness of that forest was the result of thousands of years of peaceful coexistence between man and nature. Of respect, balance, love, hope and the destiny of the earth's species.

As an adult, I came to understand that my grandad's stories about the lungs of Africa were not random. He was educating me about the value of being kind to our environment and our communities. Perhaps, to him, as an orphan of a civil war, that was the most powerful lesson he could share with his only granddaughter.

When I moved into a flat of my own for the very first time, after years of sharing houses with former roommates and two ex-boyfriends, the first thing I did was to create an indoor garden in my living room. It took some time to grow. The purpose of those plants was to keep alive the memory of my grandad's commitment to hope and community. He had already passed away a few years ago by then, and I wanted my indoor garden to give justice to his legacy.

Over time, and quite unexpectedly, my next-door neighbour's plants started to fill my living room. Milo was going on holiday for a month and he asked me to take care of them. I believe plants should never be left behind on their own, so I offered to take them in while he was away.

At the time, we were slowly starting to get to know each other. Soon he became a very important person in my life. Someone I was able to talk to, laugh with, and spend some meaningful time with, in silence. We became so close that we would organise dinners on weekends to keep each other company. I was obviously very attracted to him. One day, while his plants were still staying with me, I suddenly realised that they matched incredibly well with my indoor garden. In a strange and whimsical way, for the first time, I felt I was in love with him.

During the month he was away, I soon started missing Milo. Sometimes, I would even talk to his plants and tell them not to worry, he is coming back soon, and he will be there for you. I was obviously talking to myself too. I was scared that he might not feel the same way and that at some point I would end up with a broken heart.

While Milo was on holiday, I had a lot of time to think about our encounters. To use my intuition to try to figure out if we stood a chance in the future. He seemed a kind and thoughtful man. And we both had plenty of free time on weekends. So probably he was single, as I was, and I had no competition for him. Most importantly, his plants seemed so at home in my indoor garden, that it was almost impossible to believe our plant connection was not a sign of our own destiny. See how nice our plants look together! I used to think. Surely this had to mean something; some sort of magical sign that the love we had for each other had to be true and possible?

I knew my granddad would have agreed with me. One of his stories about the lungs of Africa spoke of how its indigenous peoples learnt to integrate nature with their intuition to understand and make sense of the world around them. The tropical flora and fauna existed for more than just breathing. They were there to tell the story of their ancestors, thereby teaching the communities to live in the present and create a future that would always protect the richness of their existence. The lungs of Africa were there to give them hope.

My indoor garden wasn't the only legacy from my granddad. I was committed to helping others and this was why I became a doctor. I wanted to save lives but doing that in a hospital in Barcelona wasn't enough for me. I wanted to help people who really needed it. So I signed on with a non-governmental organisation (NGO) expecting to get a call at some point in the next few years to travel to a conflict zone and help save the lives of those affected by humanitarian crises.

I knew that phone call had the potential to change my fate and it terrified me. But I also knew I would go for it whatever happened. The NGO told me they already had a large pool of doctors to draw from and that it could take a while, perhaps years, before I got a spot on one of their rotations.

I silently wished for the world to get better so that I would never be needed. But that wish was never granted. A few months after Milo came back from his trip, I was called up by the NGO to move to Africa to give medical care to the communities affected by the violence in the Democratic Republic of the Congo.

This time around, it was Milo who took my plants to his flat to take care of them while I was away. My trip was going to be a lot longer than his. Perhaps a year or more. I was given only a month to prepare. I spent it either getting ready to travel or trying to find the courage to let Milo know that I loved him.

We had one last dinner together before I left. And yet again I failed to share my feelings. He did not say anything either. But I could feel the same energy between us that I felt when his plants and mine were together. I kept the memory of this feeling inside me as a hope that I had a place somewhere in his heart to come back to.

My grandad was still with us at the time of the Rwandan Civil War. I remember him sitting in his living room, watching the news and almost crying, seeing yet another country go through a civil war – one of the worst genocides in human history. A few times, my grandad had said to me while pointing his finger at the TV, "Look! This is how us humans are destroying the inner peace of the lungs of Africa".

When I was a child, and in all the times he had told me stories about this forest, he never actually mentioned anything about his own life and what he had gone through during the Spanish Civil War.

At the time of the war in Rwanda I was older, and he no longer needed to hide complex and harmful information for a child. For the first time, he shared with me his belief that if we had never severed our connection with nature and the earth, killing in the name of ideologies and material desires would never have happened. To him, armed conflict was the result of very greedy power aspirations of men who, at some point, completely disconnected themselves from their communities and the natural world.

These people were chasing after more of what they already had or even needed. Their willingness to do anything to grasp power was due to their reluctance to accept that the basic things that humans and nature were able to offer each other were already enough to live comfortably in the present and develop a sustainable environment for the future.

Violence in the Democratic Republic of the Congo erupted as a result of the refugee crises triggered by Rwanda's massacre. This unresolved armed conflict, that left more than four and a half million people internally displaced, was the reason I was needed as an international doctor.

My grandad told me that the choices we make, make us who we are. And that all is lost when people lose hope. Standing in that emergency aid camp, with the blood of badly wounded children on my hands, I tried to visualise Barcelona, my indoor garden and Milo's plants. It helped calm me down and kept me from losing hope, like my grandad would have always wanted.

The way we deal with love teaches us a lot about how we deal with life. In the midst of such horror, holding onto my love for Milo helped me remember who I was, why I would love someone like him, and why he was so important to me. Through him I saw myself, as much as I saw my grandad's legacy through my indoor garden.

The humanitarian crisis I was witnessing was so unbearable that I clung to my love for Milo to survive the pain. In a way, I was grateful I never told him how I felt. If he had rejected me before I left, I would not have had his strength to keep me going during the days I spent in makeshift camps saving lives.

The hope that he was in love with me and just waiting for us both to be ready to embrace our love for each other became an inner voice that kept me safe and grounded. In the same way that I talked to his plants when he was on holiday so that they wouldn't miss him.

There was one plant, though, that never listened to me during that whole month that Milo was away. She was always sad with torn leaves. I re-potted her and tried to heal her, but with little luck. Superstitiously, I wondered if that plant was the one that was losing hope. The one that knew I was being a fool and that there would never be love between Milo and me. I wanted that plant to survive so badly. To get better, to get her leaves back.

During the year I spent in the Democratic Republic of the Congo, the love that I had for that plant was embodied in my reluctance to give up hope of the recovery of those badly wounded children. I dreamed of them leaving the camps, the armed conflict over, and becoming adults free to pursue a life of their own. In the same way my grandad did when he escaped the Spanish Civil War.

I hoped for the hate and the violence to end. That the region's peoples would be able to go back to their communities and believe in a better future again. For their aspirations never to be torn apart again by armed conflict. For love and hope to flourish. So that the lungs of Africa could go back to breathing and living in harmony with its people. A hope, like my silent love for Milo.

END

#8.The Man I Want

The first time I received a proper explanation about love and heartache I was a child and I was sitting on the back seat of my parents' car. My dad was driving, and my mom was by his side at the front. I am not sure how old I was, but I do remember it was summer and we were on vacation in the countryside. More importantly, I know for sure I was too young to understand what romantic love was.

I got my passion for music from my parents. Ever since I can remember, either at home or in the car, there's always been some good music in the background. On that particular day, the famous love song 'Angie' by The Rolling Stones was playing. My mom was singing some bits of it. She always loved that song. I remember I asked her who Angie was. The name of that woman who was deeply missed was probably one of the few words I was able to understand in English, at the time.

I was too young to comprehend romantic love either. None of the things my mom explained to me about the lyrics of that song made any sense. Heartache… what was that? And if there was such a thing… why was he still in love with her if she was gone. Why were they not together? Because they loved each other… So, why not? I can remember very clearly asking these specific questions to myself: Why are they not fighting for each other? Fighting for love? What was love anyway? Was it something worth fighting for?

Amid all the confusion, I was clear about the fact that they were over. That all the beautiful things they had together were gone, for good. What would happen next? Mike Jagger sang along halfway through the song…

Growing up, I learnt that I had to fight for my dreams, my independence. That it was always best to think with my head in order to make good decisions to grow, to get somewhere so that I would succeed. That I had to work hard to get a career, make sacrifices, take risks, make hard calls and, at some point along the way, pay a bit of attention to my heart: fall in love, build a family and all the things that come with this type of commitment.

I've witnessed a lot of people (including myself) taking chances and facing fears to grow their careers. Being brave to say 'Yes' to the unknown of unclear job opportunities; not running away from them even if these were scary. Because we were told this is what we had to do to get somewhere. However,

I have seen fewer people putting the same determination and faith into love. Too scary! We can put our entire life on the line for a job that will make us succeed, our heart is a different story. We have to keep it safe because it is all about the intuition and the feelings, and all we learn in life is to use our heads. No one likes the pain of heartache, so we better stay away from trouble. Particularly because in life, work should always come first!

It almost feels as if the promise of a good job and an employer is worth more than taking risks with the feelings we have for someone we are falling in love with. In such a context, walking away from love is a lot easier than walking away from a job.

How many times have we quit jobs for the sake of adding more variety to our CVs, compared to the numerous times we have walked away from interesting people because we were not ready yet to stop looking. We wanted to stay curious, accumulating more experiences so that we could be fully sure of what we wanted from love.

But is this how love works? Is it constant trial and error that takes us to the person we want? Do we actually ever know who the person we want is?

When our heart aches, the first thing we try to do is to focus on ourselves more. I'd dare to say, most of us bury ourselves in our work and our own interests. As if this type of inner focus will be taken away from us when we fall in love again. I guess it is all about us trying to make the most of this time, while we are heartbroken, feeling miserable, but free!

My first big love broke up with me because he was looking for something else, but he did not know what that something else would be. Just in case, he made the safe move of walking away ahead of the fear of getting stuck with someone he was not sure he wanted. My second big love left I don't know why. He did not explain it too well - or at all - but somehow I understood that it was his time to go. And that was fine. We were bored with each other, but we weren't aware of it. My third big love, though, was a completely different story. He was magic!

He entered my life unannounced. When I least wanted to find a man like him. When I wanted to be fully free and when I did not want to love anyone but my family, my friends and myself.

Because he was magic, I did not have much luck escaping him. I blamed the universe for such terrible timing. Send me a man like him when I am ready but not now! I complained…

Was the universe listening to me? I haven't figured that one out yet. All I know is that everything around us was magic. Every single interaction we had in our lives was the result of charming chance encounters. Signs of love from the universe that were constantly making me think and reconsider my feelings for him. To give up on my determination to not love him. Nina Simone put a spell on the person she loved. And she didn't care about how that person felt, because to her that person was hers. Full stop. Nina's song came into my life when I was a teenager and I started to experience how tempting love could be.

If there is something that love teaches us, it is that in life we can't control anything. Everything in life is about us and someone else. Without the other we are nothing. We know that because living in communion is essentially human. Our hearts are fed by love. We are not made to be alone, and that's ok. It doesn't make us less brave, less independent or less successful in life. However, at school they teach us otherwise. That in addition to practising the complex art of friendship and learning to work in teams, we need to prioritise obtaining good marks so that we can excel. Ideally, we should be able to be the very best in something. To be better than someone else.

While I was trying to escape the spell that my magic man had put on me, a friend of mine recommended that I date more. "Meet more men and his magic will eventually vanish", he said convinced. His recipe was simple: download a couple of dating apps and start meeting men from all walks of life. "Be practical", he added. First of all, you need to create your profile. And this will be important because such a creative process will help you clarify what are you looking for... Then, according to him, when I find someone better, I will know. "Chemistry can be built, trust me", he concluded.

And this is how I found out that looking for a person to have intimacy with online is like looking for a job. I spent hours listening to love songs while I was calculating every single detail of my profile. Which photos to choose and what to say about them and about myself. Depending on what I chose to reveal, I would attract a different type of man. So I guess planning in such a way would lead me to understand what type of man I wanted.

We tend to repeat our mistakes. We focus on what it is that they might like about us. Or how much they actually do like us. Do we fit into their ideals about love? Are we what the other person wants? But to me, as I was playing around with those dating apps, for the first time the really big question was: can I love my magic man unconditionally? And by that I meant: is my love for him measured by how much he loves me? Or is this just a form of love that is not linked to how he sees me, but to how I see myself when I am with him, regardless of everything else.

I soon came to realise that using dating apps was like browsing CVs. Profiles of random strangers recommended by algorithms that were still learning about my preferences and how their qualities would tick specific boxes. It became a meritocratic form of love. Based on concepts and not the purity and the uniqueness of the person I had in front of me. Deciding whether he was a match was becoming an intellectual act. I wasn't feeling my potential new lover at all. I was just rationally trying to decide if he was better than someone else. Or for all that mattered, if he was better than my magic man.

Bon Jovi used to grumble that there are people who give love a bad name. Roberta Flack felt as if she was being killed softly by a peculiar young boy. Blue Swede complained of being hooked on a feeling. But all I felt was that there was no sunshine when my magic man was gone, as Bill Withers would lament. Because to me, he was complete. So there we were together, my magic man and I, drinking red wine and playing some music. And for the first time, I let go and I started singing one of my favourite love songs: Peter Murphy's 'A Strange Kind of Love'. The kind of love that can either be love or hate, that makes you stay or makes you go. And that pushes you to find the truth. To make a choice, to take a chance. So that love takes on a meaning of its own.

END

I, Passing Guest

When did love become so brutal? So instrumental, so rational, so…detached from human life?

I was given once the worst advice ever: do not fall in love. Apparently, there is some sort of rule that doesn't recommend falling in love when the time is not right. Today, I am still wondering about the meaning of 'the right time to fall in love'. As if anything in life ever happens at the right time. Whoever came up with this, I'd like to have a word with that person to make it clear no one should ever put such a restraint on love. Love should always be free. Regardless, I made the mistake once of following that nonsense. At the time, I stupidly believed that this was a good recommendation. That carrying a broken heart meant I was not entitled to love for a while.

So here I am, standing on the roof of my new home in Dakar, in Senegal. It is one of those beautiful nights, when the dry breeze makes the steamy summer heat a distant memory.

The sky is clear, and I have the full moon right above my head. As I look up at the starry sky, I think of the night we first kissed under another beautiful moon, in London. On that day, I was excited to be there with you, but I was also full of sorrow and empty of hope. Other men had passed through my life. They had all left. I was so sure you would also just pass by, that I told myself this time around I would be the one breaking someone else's heart. I would never fall in love with you. I would be the one to leave. I would be the one to break your heart. I'd be your passing guest.

"It is what it is", you used to whisper in my ear when something worried me, when I was scared. It was your gentle way of saying that you were there for me. That I didn't need to worry because even though I couldn't change the issue that was perturbing me, you would hold my hand. With you, fear no longer had power over me. Your 'it is what it is' mantra taught me something very powerful: to focus on the things that kept me grounded. To rise above the unknown and to let love (your love) guide me to safety. We shared many secrets you and I, but I never told you the story behind the snake tattoo on my ankle. I almost did, many times, because I knew you were curious, but you also respected my privacy, so you never asked.

I got it done before I left Hong Kong. It was my way to ensure I would never forget the lessons I learnt there. I placed it on my ankle because it is closer to the earth and I thought it would keep me grounded when I was scared. I first held a snake when I was 12 years old. It was also the first time I faced a big fear. I had heard so many different stories about snakes: How they can eat animals in one go and just digest them; strangle people; kill you with just one bite…terrifying! And yet, I held the snake just to find how humble, sweet and soft it was. I wonder now how it took me so long to understand the lesson that the snake taught me. That fear is irrational, and most of the time it comes from a lack of answers to the things we don't know. I wish I had remembered the message hidden under the skin of my ankle before I let that stupid advice of when not to fall in love influence me, to make me scared. To protect myself from your magic.

Love and the fear of breakups are a bit like snakes. They are this interesting mix of the fear of destruction and the power of transformation. A breakup, they say, is the end of a cycle. Perhaps this is why they like to say that there are plenty of fish… plenty of people for us to take our pick. I wonder if this is one of those well-established euphemisms to get us to move on. So that we don't have to face the fear of emptiness that we experience when the other person is gone. That moment when the mystery kicks in. Then, for the first time we are left with no answers. We don't know where our ex-lover is, or with whom… are we being missed? For you and me, all the things we had some certainty about as a result of being together, are now part of the emptiness of the unknown.

I could see you through your fears and who the person was hiding behind them. Everything else, I did not need to know. I was ready to let our life together surprise me. With this realisation, I also finally let go of that self- imposed restraint on not falling in love with you. Honestly, I did not care if you didn't love me back. All I knew was that I had never met a man like you before. When I opened my heart to you, I was also able to see that you were scared of us too. Why? Is the only question I regret never asking you. Sometimes I wondered if maybe you thought you couldn't make me happy. Maybe you thought I was too intense? Maybe you thought I did not know who I was? But I did know who I was quite well… So maybe this was why you thought I was too much, intimidating even. Maybe this was why you convinced yourself you couldn't make me happy. And maybe this was the reason you left.

Breakups are an act of renunciation. There are no dissolutions without hurt. We are told to stop living in the past so that we can let go and focus on the future. But I refuse to let you go and for the first time in my life, I don't need to know. I am done with seeking answers. I am ready to live with the unknown. With you I stopped searching for what could be lost.

You were the link to my past, you became my present and I will need to wait to find out if you, this stranger who once became my lover, will one day be the man I share the rest of my life with. Call me crazy if you want, but my snake tattoo is also a reminder that there needs to be space for magic in life. So, for now, until I am ready to look elsewhere, I will keep going up to my roof in Dakar hoping you are somewhere staring at the moon and thinking about me, missing me. Finding your way back to me.

Is the moon pulling us apart or pulling us together? Regardless, I just know you will never be gone. The imprint that you left on me will grow and shrink just like the moon. But it will always be there. Because you are the best man I ever met. The first man I truly loved, and the one who took away my sorrow and filled my heart with hope. You gave me **FREEDOM.**

I LOVE YOU!

END

Why 'Passing Guest'

'Passing Guest' is the English translation of the Chinese expression 過客 (Guò Kè). It is used to describe the friends that life forces us to leave behind and how they influenced us on our journey. Inspired by the wisdom behind these words, I integrated the concept of 'Passing Guest' into my creative process. I imagined these fictional love stories as being interconnected under the idea of life as a circle (not linear); with the stories creating a circle themselves. Altogether, they form a journey where love becomes a passing guest, and the narrator becomes a passing guest herself. On top of that, as part of my creative experiment on love described in the prologue, I also played around with the idea of imagining the life of bystanders and becoming a guest in their imaginary lives and love stories, while they became temporary guests of my imagination and creativity.

Big thank you to my dear friend, Crystal Tang, for teaching me this concept, once upon a time.

(过客: Simplified Chinese characters of the traditional version above).

ANNEX

Love and Justice

Many people **Love in Silence**. It is not that they do it secretly. Simply that they have the gift of loving without expecting anything in return. They choose their loved ones **Selflessly**. Usually without defined criteria. Their intuition is profound so they can detect those who need to be loved.

Make no mistake, theirs is not a merciful duty. But an act of gratuitous affection. It is usually motivated by their acute sense of **Justice**, which alerts these privileged few to direct love towards those who need such care.

I once met a man who **Suffered in Silence**. In his case, he did so without being aware that he was hiding his suffering. He knew how to love and wanted love, but he did not know how to do it. This caused him the terrible suffering that he was shamefully hiding.

This man was also kind and honest. He was afraid of exposing his beautiful energy to others. Thus, he remained silent for a long time, years perhaps ... he had lost count. Until he unexpectedly met a woman that he was able to **Love Silently**.

She, in addition to loving, also **Suffered in Silence**. Hers was another kind of suffering. She lived with the burden of the **Injustices** that weigh on these **Righteous People** who **Love in Silence**. However, she never gave up. She continued, faithful to what her heart was dictating as being the right thing to do: to love the other. As if every time she did it, that **Compassionate Love** was becoming a blank canvas that needed to be filled in with a new type of silent love.

Her **Righteous Love** was different each time. And the impenetrable suffering that it left in her was more and more painful. But she did not give up. Neither did the man who **Suffered in Silence.** He wanted to believe that somehow there had to be a way out of all that suffering, but he could not find it. He was living in despair and with the fear of maybe giving up on himself. Or even worse, losing himself forever.

The serendipitous beauty of chance encounters made it possible for their respective sufferings to unexpectedly meet.

The woman who **Loved in Silence**, quickly noticed that she was again facing a case that required her attention. Likewise, the man who **Suffered in Silence**, soon realised that this time around he was in serious trouble. The sweetness of the woman was so great that perhaps the moment had come for him to stop **Suffered in Silence**. But he couldn't! He did not know how to do it and his suffering was exacerbated.

The woman would not give up. After all, all she did was open her heart to this man who required it so badly. She thought of him and what would help him. When they met, all she wanted was to avoid causing the man more suffering. Her ability to **Love in Silence**, allowed her to anticipate the man's needs and the things he deserved to feel loved.

The magic of the few who know how to **Love in Silence** lies in their abilities to turn even the most mundane actions into sweetness, love and affection. Many of these special **Love-Recipients** feel overwhelmed and react erratically, perpetuating their silent suffering forever.

When that happens, those who **Love in Silence** suffer the **Injustices** of the rejection of those who receive their affection. Fear keeps these **Silent Sufferers** in a circle of truths and lies that they tell themselves so that they don't have to commit to the savage act of finally overcoming and abandoning their suffering.

There are a very small number of cases in which the spell of the **Injustices** that fall upon the **Righteous** who **Love in Silence** is broken. It happens when those who **Love in Silence** are finally released from their suffering. A feat that only materialises when those who **Suffer in Silence** recognise the value of the person in front of them and are open to what the benefit is of **Loving in Silence**. In that moment, their lives change forever. Order is restored and that precious and elusive **SILENT LOVE** creates **JUSTICE.**

END

The 'There You Stay' Lady

*To my mom and two grandmas,
and to all the 'real' women
in my family.*

Have you ever regretted addressing a stranger on the street? I have, many times!

Perhaps because I am a writer, I see strangers with curiosity rather than fear. I feel remorse when I miss the chance to talk to interesting people. So I have made a rule for myself to never avoid a stranger. I came up with this rule after meeting Anthony, in London. Before that, he was yet another stranger I was ignoring, thinking that it was good to apply some self-restraint to my outgoing personality. I had been told too many times that London was a city full of crazy people. That this was not my native Hanoi, in Vietnam. And that it was best that I stayed away from people I don't know. If Anthony had ever received such advice of self-restraint, he had clearly chosen to ignore it.

"What are you reading?" he asked me this morning when we spoke for the first time.

"Something that I wrote." I cautiously replied.

That sounded interesting to him. He did not even ask me why I had written something. Clearly, he was not curious about it. Maybe he didn't even care. He got a bit closer and sat down by my side.

"Read it to me, please" he said.

This was much more than just some casual conversation. Reading to a stranger is something I would not even do in Hanoi! I thought to myself.

Anthony and I had been enjoying the sunset from the same spot at Regent's Canal, in east London, for weeks. I was curious about him, but my self-restraint prevented me from talking to him. As I ignored my inner calling, I left it all to my imagination, wondering who that African man was and why he was there by himself as often as I was. When the weather is nice and there is the promise of a good sunset, I rush to this spot to perform one of my favourite rituals: reading the last story I have written. For some reason, being there in the open, before the night falls, gives me a clarity I can't find indoors, during the day.

I started reading the title out loud to him, "The 'There You Stay Lady'." This was as far as I got. Anthony interrupted me immediately.

"Who is this lady?" he asked.

I thought he was a bit impatient, to be honest. How can he ask me to read a story and then interrupt me before I can even get to the first sentence?

I explained to him that the lady in question was my grandma. This is how my grandad used to refer to her after she passed away. My grandad was a big storyteller, and he knew a lot better than I did how to build momentum. He had a gift for this. Perhaps this was the reason why he waited until I was 16 years old, after my grandma had passed away, to tell me how he fell in love with her.

They had met at my ancestral village during a festival to worship the forebears of the big clan living in the village. My grandad never explained to me what happened on that day. Because to him, the only thing that mattered - and what he wanted me to know - was that moment in which he knew he had no way to escape her.

"There you stay!" were the last few words my grandma threw at my grandad when they had a fight a few weeks before getting married. She was pissed at him, apparently, over a dispute on the logistics of leaving the village after their wedding and moving to Hanoi to seek better opportunities. My grandma was true to her words. She walked away from that conversation in the middle of the street, and she refused to see my grandad for quite a few days. An attitude that required a lot of courage for a woman in rural Vietnam in the early 40s. All that was expected from my grandma at the time was to perform her duties as a wife and a mother.

My grandma resisted the pressure from her mom and everyone around her to go back to my grandad. She was convinced it was he who had to apologise. My grandad's family obviously thought otherwise. They were worried about his reputation if he bowed down to my grandma's behaviour, which he did. He knew he couldn't lose someone like her. She mattered too much to him! By trying to get her back, he also earned the respect of my grandma, as well as her heart. Even if that cost him the support of his family.

When my grandad shared this story with me, I realised that my grandma's words "there you stay" embodied all she was as a woman; beyond everyone else's expectations. And that included her dreams for herself and the type of man she wanted to marry. When she passed away, all that my grandad wanted to remember about her was the woman that she was before they married; before she became a mother and a grandmother. He remembered the independent, free woman only he had the chance to know. After that, she became just a mother and a grandmother. And all that was left of that free spirit stayed within the privacy of my grandma and the moments she shared only with my grandad, as a woman and as a lover.

When my granddad missed her, which happened very often, he would say to me: "The 'there you stay lady'"… wait for me in heaven until I am ready to come and join you. In the meantime, I'll be staying with our family. They still need me here."

Since the day he shared that story with me, my granddad stopped calling her grandma in front of me. Only to him and me, she was The 'there you stay lady'. A nickname that he refused to share with anyone else.

A couple of years after my grandma's passing, when I turned 18 years old, I came to London to study and I never went back to Vietnam. My last visit to Hanoi was just a few months ago, and that was the last time I had the chance to see my grandad smiling and saying to me: "The 'there you stay lady', keep waiting for me. They still need me here."

And she did wait for him, until he passed away yesterday, on the same day my boyfriend broke up with me. Anthony interrupted me and asked, "So you feel you did not honour the legacy that your grandad passed onto you from The 'there you stay lady'… This is why you wrote this story. You are blaming yourself for not showing the woman you are to this boyfriend who ran away on the day you lost your grandad."

I nodded. He had figured it out. I had nothing else to say.

Anthony quickly broke the silence as he tried to explain that this was not the reason my ex left. Apparently, Anthony's mom shared some good storytelling talents with my grandad. However, Anthony's memory was not as good as mine. He tried to excuse himself by raising the fact that he wasn't a writer, as he shared the moral of a fable his mom told him when he met his wife. Anthony's mom had chosen to move back to Lagos, in Nigeria, when his dad passed away. As an immigrant, she preferred to live closer to her roots when she became a widow. Consequently, when Anthony was thinking of getting married, his mom wasn't there for him, in person.

He had forgotten the full story that his mom had told him when he thought he had made a mistake that would take his future wife away from him forever. This is the only thing that stayed with him: "If you love each other, love will never be lost. Whatever happens, you will always find a way back to each other."

Anthony believed I had misunderstood my grandma's legacy. And that I had made no mistake. Love wasn't about my proving myself to anyone, playing games or being persuasive. Love meant finding someone who was able to fall in love with the woman I was.

"Real love is never lost", he concluded.

"Are you alone? What happened with that woman that was supposed to become your wife?" I asked him.

"We got married, but I have just lost my real love" he answered.

"What? Why? You have just told me real love is never lost!" I exclaimed.

"Well, there is an exception", Anthony said. "When you close your eyes to the real person you have in front of you. And you don't want to see how lucky you are to have real love in front of you… then real love is lost."

He took a little pause, before he continued, "I did not want to see the real woman I had in front of me, even though she was there to see me. Eventually she slowly faded away, until I lost her."

I interrupted him quickly, "Wait a second Anthony, your sunset ritual… you are coming here to see your mom! Did she pass away recently and now that she is gone, do you think you owe her?"

He nodded as he shared, "I wonder if my dad ever saw her as the real woman she was. We, her children, failed at doing that. To us she was just our mom. So I am determined to come here every day when there is a beautiful sunset, to honour her as the woman she was and I never met."

END

NOTE ON THE 'THERE YOU STAY LADY': This short story was originally published on my blog. I wrote it to commemorate the International Women's Day and the Women's History Month, on March 2021.

Main Language

Recently I had to fill out some official forms and I was asked what my main language was. Apparently - and according to their definition of 'main language' - mine would be the one that came naturally to mind first. They never mentioned anything about that language being my mother tongue or something similar. Honestly, I did not know what to answer.

For me, that I speak more than one language fluently, it is hard to say if there is one that stands out. To start with, I grew up in a bilingual environment speaking Catalan and Spanish as my two mother tongues. On top of that, in my family and with a lot of friends, we usually mix and match the two languages in many casual conversations. Even at work, depending on who the stakeholders are, we constantly switch from Catalan to Spanish, holding interesting bilingual conversations.

Later, when I moved abroad, Chinese and English became the two other languages that are now a big part of my life and my identity. The four of them, altogether, come to my mind first in different situations and different contexts. Most of the time, it is a subconscious reflex. I find my lack of rigidity in the use of a particular language one of the most beautiful things of my life.

As a writer, language also affects the flavour of my creative process. Of my two mother tongues, Spanish is the one that my creativity associates with storytelling: I grew up listening to the fantasy tales that my grandad shared with me always in Spanish, his native language. This is surely when my mind associated Spanish as my main language for storytelling, instead of Catalan. This is also a beautiful legacy from my grandad; writing in Spanish always reminds me of him.

Unfortunately, my written Chinese is not fluent enough to write stories at this level. Over the years living away from Spain, English is the language that has become my main language for a lot of things, including some of my storytelling.

There are stories that come to my mind in English first, others in Spanish. The language in which they come alive affect my point of view on them and the world that I create around those words.

Passing Guest is a collection of stories that germinated in my imagination in English, and so this is the language in which they were written.

Acknowledgements

"London is a very unkind and tough city", I was warned when I moved to the United Kingdom. Either they were all wrong or there are two Londons. And I was lucky enough to tap into the one that is loving and kind.

I want to thank everyone who proved that warning to be wrong. All the people who showed me the kindness and love that London has to offer, beyond any stereotypes or predetermined norms and conditionings. Some were passing guests, others stayed in my life in different ways. There were random strangers too who were inadvertently kind, and who made my landing in this new environment gentler. Small or big, their acts of love and kindness were crucial to my first years in London. I can't name them all here, but they all hold the same importance for me.

Below are the names of a few people I'd like to highlight for what they meant at the personal level both in London and beyond. For making my life kinder while I was moving countries.

I want to make a special mention to my friend Robbie R. for his compassion, honesty and kindness. The lockdowns would have been a lot harder without having you downstairs.

And to Rachel, for taking care of me. Thanks for sharing your magical wisdom about life with me and making me feel less alone.

Heather G., thanks for giving me an opportunity that opened up a life full of new possibilities in London.

I would also like to mention the kindness, compassion and care of my clients who have been supporting and following my journey in London and beyond in real life before the pandemic and online during lockdowns. Particularly, to my movement community for trusting me with their wellbeing journey and for inspiring me to keep growing, even during such a tough time for everyone.

Last but not least, I am grateful to the From a Future and Posit Place Design & Tech community in Hong Kong and around the world with whom I publicly shared this creative experiment and the vision behind *Passing Guest*, for the first time.

And of course, this book would not have been possible without the love of all the members of my family, including my parents and grandparents, without whom I wouldn't be who I am today. As well as my beloved Mediterranean and the experiences I carry in my heart from the many years I spent living in Asia.

Ahmed M.

Ahmed S.

Alex P.

Alison H.

Andrea R.

Anja F.

Auston D.

Cecilia M.

Clara L.

Dina S.

Dorota S.

Florence del P.

Indrit S.

Iris S.

Isa-Welly L.

Jen K.

Josep Maria B.

Magali L.

Marc M.

Mariona S.

Marta M.

Marta P

Nacho C. i les nenes, Lola i Vera

Nandita S.

Nelson O.

Noel L.

Patricia A.

Roberto R.

Rosie J.

Silvia G.

Stuart T.

Susana L.

Xavier M.

Xavi R.

Yanitsa D.

Yi Yan Ch.

About the Author

Iris Mir (Barcelona, 1983) has a Bachelors of Sciences degree in Communication Sciences from Ramon Llull University and a Master's degree in Political Science, specialising in new models of democracy and an Executive Education Course in Management and Leadership Development from the Business School at Westminster University. She is also a certified ScrumMaster©.

Sharing stories has been a constant in Iris' professional career. This passion has taken different forms throughout the many years she lived in Hong Kong and Beijing, first as an international correspondent for Spanish and international media and later as an expert in communication and cross-cultural project management in Asia and Europe.

The exposure to different Asian cultures and lifestyles nurtured her passion for exploring creativity, personal identity and self-expression beyond the conventional methods of communication. These experiences brought her closer to the worlds of dance and movement. Currently, she lives in London and focuses her professional activity on cultural diversity, identity, self-expression and creativity through writing, masterclasses at universities, talks, workshops and MindBody programmes.

Iris dreams of a future of sustainable innovation, where all communities have space to use their own voices and co-create alternative futures

For all the latest news from Iris Mir, sign up for her newsletter at www.irismir.net

南楓樓

The Mansion
South of Maple Street

Sham Shui Po, Hong Kong

Iris Mir

The Mansion South of Maple Street

Sham Shui Po, Hong Kong

"When you go out, meet with honorable people" 出路遇貴人

A thirty-something Mediterranean woman moves to Hong Kong, where she is welcomed by the honourable community of residents of the traditional neighbourhood of Sham Shui Po. Through them, she discovers the true meaning of hope in an environment where imagination and the dreams of a better life have influenced the choices of the people of Hong Kong and their ancestors.

The Mansion South of Maple Street exposes the plurality of identities and the existential experiences that coexist in Hong Kong and which demonstrate the complexities of life as an immigrant.

Inspired by true events, this intimate novel reveals a Hong Kong that, like the protagonist herself, is trying to find itself.

Through the voice of the narrator and the stories of the residents of Sham Shui Po, Iris Mir explores the value of questioning worlds and possibilities in order to invent and shape transgressive options for the future that stand as alternatives to a finite truth.